Six White Boomers

Rolf Harris was always amazed that in his home town of Perth, Christmas temperatures reached over thirty degrees Celsius, yet they were singing songs about Christmas in the snow. As a result, he and a friend, John D Brown, set out to write something that would capture the difference about Christmas in Australia, when there's no snow, and reindeers are found only in zoos. The idea of swapping reindeers for big, old-man kangaroos, led to this unique Christmas song, which was an immediate success when first released in 1960 and has now become a classic.

Six White Boomers

Written by
Rolf Harris & John D Brown

Illustrated by
Bruce Whatley

A Margaret Hamilton book
from
Scholastic Australia

Early on one Christmas Day a Joey kangaroo

Was far from home and lost

in a great big zoo.

Up beside the bag of toys, little Joey hopped.

But they hadn't gone far when Santa stopped,

Unharnessed all the reindeer

and Joey wondered why.

Then he heard a far off booming in the sky.

Six white boomers, snow white boomers,
Racing Santa Claus through the blazing sun.
Six white boomers, snow white boomers,
On his Australian run.

Pretty soon old Santa
began to feel the heat,
Took his fur-lined boots off
to cool his feet.

Into one popped Joey, feeling quite okay
While those old man kangaroos
kept pulling on the sleigh.

Six white boomers, snow white boomers,

Racing Santa Claus through the blazing sun.

Six white boomers, snow white boomers,

On his Australian run.

Joey said to Santa,
'Santa, what about the toys?
Aren't you giving some
to these girls and boys?'

They've all got their presents, Son,
We were here last night.
This trip is an extra trip,
Joey's special flight.'

Six white boomers, snow white boomers,

Racing Santa Claus through the blazing sun.

Six white boomers,

snow white boomers,

On his Australian run.

Soon the sleigh was flashing past,
right over Marble Bar.

'Slow down there,' cried Santa.

'It can't be far.'

'Come up on my lap here, Son,
and have a look around.'

'There she is, that's Mummy,
bounding up and down.'

Six white boomers, snow white boomers,
Racing Santa Claus through the blazing sun.

Six white boomers, snow white boomers,

On his Australian run.

Well that's the bestest Christmas treat
that Joey ever had,
Curled up in mother's pouch
feeling snug and glad.

The last they saw was Santa
heading northward from the sun,
The only year the boomers
worked a double run.

Six white boomers, snow white boomers,
Racing Santa Claus through the blazing sun.

Six white boomers,
snow white boomers

On his Australian run.

First published in 2001 by Margaret Hamilton Books
PO Box 28, Hunters Hill NSW 2110 Australia
an imprint of Scholastic Australia Pty Ltd
PO Box 579, Gosford NSW 2250.
www.scholastic.com.au

Copyright © text, Rolf Harris and John D Brown, 2001. Copyright © illustrations, Bruce Whatley, 2001.
Cover photograph of Rolf Harris, copyright © Chris Christodoulou.
National Library of Australia Cataloguing-in-publication entry
Harris, Rolf, 1930- . Six white boomers. ISBN 1 876289 60 0.
I. Whatley, Bruce. II. Brown, John D. III. Title. A823.3

Bruce Whatley used watercolours for the illustrations.

Typeset in Spumoni.
Printed in Singapore by Imago.
10 9 8 7 6 5 4 3 2 1   1 2 3 4 5 / 0